DOZY MARE

Jeanne Willis and Tony Ross

Andersen Press•London

For Gill Hanlon - J.W.

Text copyright © 2005 by Jeanne Willis. Illustrations copyright © 2005 by Tony Ross.
The rights of Jeanne Willis and Tony Ross to be identified as the author and illustrator of this work
have been asserted by them in accordance with the Copyright, Designs and Patents Act, 1988.
First published in Great Britain in 2005 by Andersen Press Ltd., 20 Vauxhall Bridge Road, London SW1V 2SA.
Published in Australia by Random House Australia Pty., 20 Alfred Street, Milsons Point, Sydney, NSW 2061.
All rights reserved. Colour separated in Switzerland by Photolitho AG, Zürich.
Printed and bound in Italy by Grafiche AZ, Verona.

10   9   8   7   6   5   4   3   2   1

British Library Cataloguing in Publication Data available.

ISBN 1 84270 386 2

This book has been printed on acid-free paper

Once, there was a very lazy horse . . .

All she ever did was stand still.
All day. Every day.

Except on Sunday.
She never stood still on Sunday . . .

She sat down instead.

"Giddy up, you dozy mare!"
said the farmer.
But the horse wouldn't.
"Giddy up yourself," she said.

She wouldn't go forwards.
She wouldn't go back.
Not even for a carrot.

She just stood there.

So the farmer gave the horse to his wife.
"Trot on, you dozy mare!" she said.
"Trot off, you hefty lump!" said the horse.
She wouldn't go left.
She wouldn't go right.
Not even for some oats.
She just stood there.

So the wife gave the horse to her son.
"Hi ho, Silver!" yelled the boy.
"Ho hum, sonny," yawned the horse.

She wouldn't play cowboys.
She wouldn't play ball.
Not even for an apple.
She just stood there.

So the son gave the horse to his sister.
"Jump, you dozy mare!" she said.
"Jump yourself!" said the horse.
She wouldn't jump high.
She wouldn't jump low.
Not even for a sugar lump.
She just stood there.

So the sister sold the horse to a tinker.
"Pull my cart, you dozy mare!" he said.
"Pull it yourself!" said the horse.
She wouldn't pull.
She wouldn't push.
Not for all the hay in Hampshire.
She just stood there.

So the tinker sold the horse to a circus.
"Dance, you dozy mare!" said the ringmaster.
"Not to *your* tune," said the horse.
She wouldn't dance.
She wouldn't prance.
Not even for an ice cream.
She just stood there.

So the ringmaster sold the horse to a butcher.
"Stand still, you dozy mare!" he said.
But the mare wasn't half as dozy as people thought.
"Not flipping likely!" she said.

She wouldn't stand still,
She wouldn't sit down.
Not even for a second —

She ran like the wind . . .

Giddy up, giddy up!
Forwards and back,
Left and right,
Hi ho!

Jumping and playing,
Pulling and pushing,
Prancing and dancing,
All the way to . . .

. . . Freedom!